Cassie, You're a Winner!

Renée Kent

ADVENTURES IN MISTY FALLS

1

Cassie, You're a Winner!

Renée Kent

New Hope® Publishers

Birmingham, Alabama

New Hope® Publishers
P.O. Box 12065
Birmingham, AL 35202-2065
www.newhopepubl.com

Library of Congress Cataloging-in-Publication Data

Kent, Renée, 1955-
Cassie, you're a winner! / Renee Kent.
    p. cm. -- (Adventures in Misty Falls ; 1)
Summary: Because she needs to be best at something, Cassie hopes to win several blue ribbons at the Misty Falls Fair where she learns that with God, she is always a winner.
  ISBN 1-56309-735-4
[1. Christian life--Fiction.
2. Competition (Psychology)--Fiction.
3. Fairs--Fiction.]
 I. Title. PZ7.K419
Cas 2000 [Fic]--dc21 99-050658

Cover design by Todd Cotton
Cover illustration by Matt Archambault

ISBN: 1-56309-735-4
N007116 • 0400 • 7.5M1

Cassie, You're a Winner!

1

Upside down and inside out. Cassie's stomach felt just like that, as the motion of the Tumbler spun her high over the Misty Falls Fairgrounds.

With her best friend J.J. bumping and giggling alongside, Cassie's auburn ponytail flipped and swirled with each crazy turn and twist. She tried to brace herself against the safety bar to avoid sliding into J.J., but that was quite impossible. In fact, Cassie found herself sitting in J.J.'s lap as the Tumbler thrust them to one side, then abruptly changed directions.

The girls squealed with delight and maybe just a little fear—the fun kind. As the girls slid and swayed from side to side, the downy feathers and colorful beads in J.J.'s hair clasp tickled Cassie's nose.

"Phnew!" Cassie sneezed.

"God bless you!" hollered J.J. over the grinding roar of the fair ride.

"What?" cried Cassie, holding onto her stomach.

Adventures in Misty Falls

Springfield

Illinois

Indiana

Ohio

West Virginia

Kentucky

Virginia

Nashville

North Carolina

Memphis

Tennessee

Charlott

Misty Falls

Columbia

Birmingham

Atlanta

South Carolina

Jackson

Montgomery

Georgia

Mississippi

Alabama

Tallahassee

Jacksonville

New Orleans

Louisiana

Florida

Gulf of Mexico

Orlando

Tampa

Saint Petersburg

Cassie, You're a Winner!

"I said—oh, never mind!" squealed J.J. as the ride turned them upside down again.

Every time the pair expected the ride might slow down, the spinning grew faster. Cassie barely noticed the sharp pain of J.J.'s fingernails digging into her arm. She was too busy trying to tightly grasp the safety bar. All the while, the girls' laughter was just as out of control as the Tumbler itself.

Above all the fair commotion below, Cassie was celebrating with extra zeal. Today was even more exciting to her than Christmas Eve, when her family always gathered by the Christmas tree to read the Christmas story and then open one present each.

For such a long time, a whole year, she had waited for the finest country fair in all of Georgia to arrive. And now, finally, it was here! Cassie quivered with excitement.

Cassie's dad always said that Fair Week was the only time of year when anyone noticed Misty Falls. Mother had recently said, as she studied the old crumpled map in Dad's pickup truck, "Misty Falls is so small, it's missing! It isn't even a tiny dot on the official Georgia state map!"

It was true. Cassie's hometown was just a small farm community lost somewhere outside the busy suburbs of Atlanta, the state capital of Georgia.

Richmond

Raleigh

But when it came time each year for the Misty Falls Fair, people traveled to town from all over the place, and Cassie knew it.

She simply had the most amazing feeling that this year was going to be her year to shine at the fair. This summer she would win her first blue ribbon ever! Already, she could imagine her name on the front page of the paper in bold, black letters—**Cassie Holbrook Wins Blue Ribbons!** Everyone in Misty Falls would know that Cassie was a winner.

Up to this point, Cassies' life had been a bit too ordinary for her. She always did average work in school. She wasn't best pals with the popular kids. She just didn't feel like people noticed her, even in her own family. Unlike her parents and older brothers and sisters, Cassie had never even come close to winning or excelling at anything before. Her big claim to fame was being the "baby" in the Holbrook family.

Cassie's mom was one of the best cooks in Misty Falls, and she had taught Cassie lots over the past year. Cassie was also doing really well riding her pony, Chester. That's how she knew that by the week's end, the "baby's" ordinary image would change!

So with blue ribbons in her dreams and all the assorted swishing and swirling fair rides that her tummy could take, Cassidy Marie Holbrook celebrated the secret that her fair entries (her very special cookies and her horseback riding) would launch her into a welcome new life of fame and success.

Cassie, You're a Winner!

She just couldn't wait to see her name in the newspaper headlines and hear it announced on the radio! From this week on, Cassie silently vowed to never look back at her old humdrum life again.

As the Tumbler finally slowed to a halt, J.J. stopped giggling long enough to inhale a big gulp of air. Her mysterious indigo eyes grew wider as she exclaimed, "That was fun! You wanna ride it again?"

Cassie stared at her friend in disbelief. "I think I'll sit this one out. My tummy feels like it's jumping out of my throat!"

"Mmmm, I smell cotton candy," said J.J. with her nose in the air. "Let's get some!"

Cassie laughed and faked a groan at the same time. She tried to hold her head still. She was sure it was going to roll right off her shoulders. "You've got to be kidding," Cassie moaned. "Are you really hungry? I never want to eat again."

J.J. snickered and fondly poked her friend. "Now I know that's not true." Everybody knew that Cassie Holbrook never missed a meal, especially one with sweets in it.

When the attendant unlocked the safety door, the girls tumbled dizzily out of the Tumbler. They wobbled unsteadily toward a park bench next to the ticket sales booth. Cassie and J.J. plopped down hard on the bench at the same time. They were glad to be still for a moment. Catching her breath, Cassie watched J.J. tuck thick strands of dark hair behind her ears that sparkled with silver earrings. On J.J.'s left cheek, the tiny rainbow that a face painter had applied was smudged, but that didn't matter. Even with yellow, orange and purple smudges and smears on her face, J.J. was the prettiest girl in Misty Falls. Originally from Arizona, J.J. looked like a Native American princess.

For a moment, Cassie wished she could be Native American like J.J., because her best friend had the loveliest bronze complexion. Cassie's own skin was as white as chalk and dotted with prickly bumps. For as long as she could remember, those bumps on her arms and legs seemed to get redder and bumpier on hot days like today. Sometimes Cassie felt like a plucked chicken.

Never mind, she thought, brushing away the troublesome thought. Today was too special to waste any time thinking about her "chicken skin."

This week, she was going to become a blue ribbon winner, just like J.J.

"That was fun!" exclaimed J.J. as she bent down to pull up her socks. "Whew, the Tumbler is awesome!" As J.J. looked up, she grinned and pointed ahead.

"Look, we're about to become famous!"

Striding toward them came freckle-faced, lanky-legged Iggy Potts, framing the two girls through the lens of his trusty camera. The early afternoon sun glistened in his curly red hair and made his head appear to be on fire.

Cassie, You're a Winner!

"Say 'cheese dip,'" said Iggy, snapping one photo after another.

"Cheese dip!" sang the girls as they laughed.

Smiling for Iggy was always easy. He reminded Cassie of a real-life cartoon character. After posing using their regular smiles, they scrunched up their noses and made silly faces at the camera. "Perfect, for hams, that is," teased Iggy. Then he focused his full attention on his prized camera. It really belonged to his father, who owned a photography shop where Iggy worked each summer. Iggy was already a skilled photographer, and one day he wanted to be a professional.

Sticking out his tongue while he concentrated, he carefully used a special cloth to clean the dust off the camera lens. Afterwards, he returned his equipment to its case, which was strapped over his broad, bony shoulder.

J.J. and Cassie exchanged looks and giggled. Iggy was funny without even trying.

After a brief pause, Iggy looked confused. "Say, Cassie, what are you still doing here, anyway?" he asked. "I thought you would be home baking those stinky poodles this afternoon."

"What?" J.J. asked, breaking into a fresh round of giggles.

Iggy cleared his throat. "You know, those stinky poodle, whatcha-ma-call-em cookies. You know, for your fair exhibit tomorrow afternoon."

Cassie took great pleasure in correcting him. "You mean Snickerdoodles, not stinky poodles," she said. "Anyway, they aren't like any other cookie you've ever tasted. I have concocted my own special recipe. I call them Cassie's Snickerdoodles Deluxe."

"Well," said Iggy, rolling his eyes, "whatever they are called, when are you going to bake them? I don't think the judges want to eat flour and raw eggs."

"Ooooooh," squealed J.J. with a shiver.

"For your information," said Cassie firmly, "I'm going to bake them tonight." She didn't feel like being teased anymore. "Just you wait and see, Iggy Potts. My Snickerdoodles will be so fresh, so mouth-watering, so beautiful, that the judges will award me the first prize blue ribbon."

J.J. put her hand on Cassie's shoulder. "I can't wait, Cassie," said J.J. "So have you already groomed your trusty steed for tomorrow morning's horse show?"

At the thought of Chester, Cassie grew more excited. "Oh J.J., you should see him! My pony is squeaky clean. He's so clean, my dad says we could probably eat a hamburger off his backside."

"No thanks," said Iggy, sticking out his tongue. Both girls giggled.

Then Cassie continued. "I even polished his hooves with black polish."

Iggy laughed. "Now I've heard it all. A horse getting his nails polished."

Cassie, You're a Winner!

J.J. scolded Iggy. "Will you stop making jokes out of everything Cassie says? This horse show is a big deal."

"Sorry," said Iggy sheepishly.

"That's okay," said Cassie cheerfully. "Anyway, I spent all morning grooming Chester for his big show tomorrow. I can't wait for you both to see him. You know, it is going to be pretty exciting to show Chester in the morning and then have the cookie exhibit in the afternoon. By tomorrow night, I'll have matching blue ribbons!"

J.J. smiled and hugged her friend. "Hey! You could wear them as a new set of earrings, for special occasions."

"Now who's making jokes?" teased Iggy.

Cassie laughed, but inside she didn't think her friends could really understand how important it was for her to be best at something. But somehow, that didn't matter. This time tomorrow, she would claim victory, and her whole blue ribbon world would rejoice with her!

2

The hot afternoon sun prompted Iggy to wipe his brow. "Whew! What we need are sodas. Who's with me?" he asked, making his way to the nearest refreshment stand.

The three were soon propped against a shade tree, sipping on lemon-lime drinks. "Ah, this is the life," said J.J. as she adjusted the silver and blue bangle bracelets on her arm.

Cassie sighed dreamily. Iggy just kept slurping his soda until it was all gone. Then he said suddenly, "You know, now I'm hungry. I could use one of those stinky poodles right about now."

The girls laughed. Cassie corrected him again. "Snickerdoodles, Iggy. Is that so hard to remember?"

"So how do you make a...uh...smacky-noodle...a sticky streudel...oh you know, those famous cookies you like to bake so much?" he asked, smacking his lips.

"You're pathetic," said Cassie. "Snickerdoodles are made with pure butter, eggs, sugar, cinnamon, and stuff like that. The most important thing is to add just a slight bit of cream of tartar. That makes the cookie dough light and creamy."

"You mean like tartar that sticks on your teeth if you don't brush?" asked Iggy. "Ooh, I don't want any of your cookies if they have tooth decay in them."

J.J. rolled her eyes. "Now you are getting ridiculous, Iggy. Tell him, Cassie."

"Iggy, my patience is wearing thin with you," said Cassie, secretly quoting her mother. "Cream of tartar is not scraped off your teeth. It comes in a little jar in the grocery store. It's on a shelf near the sugar and spices."

"Okay, forget I asked. See if I eat one of your stinky poodles or whatever they are," said Iggy. He sniffed the air. "Mmm, maybe I'll just get a hot dog."

"Boys," muttered Cassie as she rolled her hazel eyes.

"Girls," muttered Iggy. "Aw, come on, Cass. What's the big deal? It's just a dumb old cookie. Why do you want that blue ribbon so badly? I've won dozens of them in photography. Who cares?"

Cassie wasn't quite sure how to answer. It was quite risky to answer honestly. After all, she didn't want her dearest friends to laugh at her and think that she was just being silly.

Finally, after a long silence, she took a deep breath and chose her words carefully. "I guess I just want to be the best at something, like the two of you."

"Oh Cassie, what are you talking about?" asked J.J.,

giving her friend a hug. "You're my best friend. See? You already are best at something—best at being my best friend."

"Thanks, J.J., but you know what I mean," said Cassie.

"No," J.J. said, wrinkling her eyebrows so that they met in the middle of her forehead. "I don't understand."

Cassie sighed. "Well, I'm not good with a camera like you are, Iggy. That's your special talent. You've been winning blue ribbons year after year."

Iggy had a mischievous look in his eyes, as if he expected an adoring crowd to gather at any moment. "I am quite a photographer, aren't I?"

Cassie playfully nudged his elbow and chuckled. "And J.J.," she continued, "You're the smartest, prettiest girl in Misty Falls—even more beautiful than the older girls in my sister's high school. Plus, you're the best horseback rider in our club."

J.J. seemed embarrassed by the compliment. For a moment, her face blushed a deeper bronze. She bowed her head until her hair fell forward and hid her eyes. "Thank you, Cassie. Now don't say anything more about me. You're special too!"

"Well, as for me," said Cassie, "I'm just an average student with average looks leading an average life. In my family, I'm just known as the 'baby' of five children."

"But you're no baby!" exclaimed Iggy. "You're practically grown up."

"To my parents and my brothers and sisters, I am a baby," complained Cassie. In my family, I'm the only one who doesn't have a special talent or ability. Mom has her cooking and a sewing business. Dad has his woodworking shop, and he's one of the best farmers in Georgia. My brother Jeff was born to play football. Sid is a lawyer. My sisters are cheerleaders and are in every play and musical that comes along. They can do everything from painting to gymnastics to car racing. But who am I? Just average, old Cassie."

J.J. stood in objection. "But Cass, you are good at a lot of things, too. You can do just about anything you try. Why, just look at how much you've learned after just one year of horseback riding!"

"Sure, how to trot and how to whoa. Big deal," said Cassie, rolling her eyes.

"It is a big deal," J.J. argued. "Cass, this is your first horse show. You can't expect to be the best at something that you are just now learning."

"But J.J., I want to be the best in my beginner class at the horse show. You are best in your advanced class, and I'm proud of you for that," said Cassie, grinning at her best friend. "If we were in the same class in the horse show, I wouldn't have a chance. But I intend to win the blue ribbon for my competition tomorrow."

J.J. looked serious, almost angry. "But Cass, I don't go into a show competing against anyone. Mainly, I just go out there and have fun."

Cassie, You're a Winner!

Cassie smiled. "Thanks for caring, J.J. I'm glad to have a friend like you. But I don't think you understand. I'm going to be twelve years old in a few months, and I've never done anything special. It's about time that I prove to myself that I am blue ribbon material. My pony Chester and I just have to do best in our class. And my Snickerdoodles will be a sure winner."

Iggy stood up, clapped his hands, and bowed deeply before Cassie. "Here's to the Stinky Poodle Queen," he said. "May your cookies rise to fame and fortune. And may Your Majesty ride like the wind upon your noble steed, Chester."

"Oh brother, just what I need! A court jester!" Cassie teased back.

J.J. glanced at her watch. "Oops, we've got to check on our horses, Cass! It's time to feed them. Oh, Iggy, don't forget that our horse shows are tomorrow morning. You're coming to cheer Cass and me on, aren't you?

"I'll be there with my camera ready," said Iggy. "You know what? I've got to get my photographs delivered to the art building. Judging begins soon. See ya later!"

As Iggy raced toward the art pavilion, he stirred up so much red dust that the girls spewed and sputtered their way toward the barns. This time tomorrow, Cassie thought, they would all be blue-ribbon winners. Cassie could just imagine a picture of the three of them on the front page of the *Misty Falls Gazette*, with the words "Champions Take First Place at Fair!"

She couldn't wait!

3

All the way to the barn, the girls chattered about their old pal, Iggy. They agreed that having a name like Franklin Ignatius (*Ig-nay-shus*) Potts, Jr. had to be tough on a person. But somehow, it fit him just right.

J.J. and Cassie turned for a moment and watched Iggy's fiery-red hair bob through the streams of fair-goers. "You know, Iggy's name really is a perfect match for his funny personality," said J.J. "He's a clown at heart."

"I know what you mean," said Cassie. "Remember the big news flash at school, when everyone found out Ignatius is his middle name?"

"Yeah! We all started calling him Iggy instead of Frank. He blushed a hundred shades of red. But after that, he didn't even seem to mind," answered J.J.

"Maybe because it made him famous. Nobody ever noticed him before," said Cassie. "But who could not notice Iggy? He sticks out in a crowd alright."

The girls couldn't help chuckling as they jogged into the welcome, cool shadows of the barn. They stood still for a moment while their eyes adjusted to the drastic light change.

What a relief to be out of the sun. A giant electric fan on the far side of the barn whipped up a breeze that smelled of fresh hay, wood shavings, and polished leather.

"Where is Gracie's stall?" asked Cassie, glancing around.

"There she is—the second one to the right," said J.J., pointing proudly. "By the way, I reserved the stall next to Gracie's for your pony. See? Your name and entry number are posted on the stall door."

"Oh thanks! I'm glad that Chester will be in one of the newer stalls," said Cassie with relief. "They're built sturdier than the older ones on the other side of the barn. You know how Chester tends to get restless and tries to escape."

The girls laughed, remembering the time Cassie's dad had to replace some boards in one wall of Chester's stall, where he had kicked himself free. But that was a long time ago. Chester was an obedient pony now.

Cassie watched as Gracie dipped her muzzle into the water for a long drink. J.J. grabbed a brush to touch up her mare's silky mane and tail.

Then J.J. peered into Gracie's water bucket. "Oops! I didn't give you enough water this morning. Sorry, girl," said J.J. She patted her chestnut mare's forehead, just above her white star marking. Gracie loved the attention.

While J.J. filled Gracie's bucket with fresh water, Cassie began to notice that almost everyone else had already brought their horses to the fairgrounds. In a sudden rush of thought, she realized that she had not made arrangements for her dad to haul Chester in the horse trailer to the fair! Cassie's pony was still at home in the barn. But at least he was clean and ready for tomorrow morning's show.

Cassie glanced at the clock in the barn. It was hard to read the time with all the spider webs and dust masking the face of the clock. Five o'clock already. The time had come to go home. With a quick explanation and good-bye to J.J., Cassie was on her way.

The more Cassie thought about all that she had to do to get ready, the faster she walked toward the bike rack. Past the main gate, she ran to her bike and pedaled as quickly as she could all the way back to her family's farm, three-and-a-half miles away.

When she got home, she bypassed the house and went straight to the barn. She hopped off her bike. Quickly, she dashed into the barn that her father had built just last year to replace the old rickety one. Flipping on the lights, she went to Chester's stall with a flake of hay and a scoop of grain—his favorite.

"Here you go buddy. Eat up, 'cause we're leaving for

the fairgrounds as soon as I can find Dad. Chester? Chester!" Cassie could hardly believe what her eyes were telling her.

The stall door was open and Chester was gone! But it couldn't be! She remembered fastening the door before she left for the fairgrounds that morning.

Oh, maybe Dad is loading him in the horse trailer, she thought hopefully. But his truck was gone and the trailer was still parked in its spot next to the barn. After following Chester's hoofprints through the barn and out to the south field, Cassie decided he must be helping himself to some green grass.

Where is that lead rope? she asked herself, digging through her tack boxes with no success. She scanned the series of hooks suspended from the ceiling in the tack room. Finally, she discovered one end of the black lead rope hidden under a bale of hay that Chester must have pulled off the loft above.

"That stupid pony," mumbled Cassie. She ran over the hill straight to where Chester liked to graze.

"Chester! Come here, boy!" she called. He was nowhere in sight. She listened for Chester's reply for a moment, which was a low nickering sound that he made when he thought she might have grain to eat. But there was no response, except for Opie, the family's Jack Russell terrier. He was busy chasing off a barn cat who had gotten too close to the house.

Cassie tromped up and down the length and width

of the field. No Chester. She searched in all of his favorite spots twice, but Chester wasn't in any of them. With each step, Cassie was growing more and more irritated.

Not only that, her throat was so dry that she decided to take the path to the spring. She made her way to the rocks that marked the spring's head, cupped her hand, and took a sip of the cool water that bubbled out of the ground. Mmm, better than her favorite soda at the fair. She looked around as she sipped, scanning the brushy area for Chester. As she stood up and looked downstream, there in the dark, moist soil was a fresh hoofprint.

"It looks like I'm not the only one who got thirsty," Cassie said aloud.

Now she knew she was on the right track, and the water had refreshed her attitude. So on she went, pushing the limbs of bushes out of the way, following the hoofprints along the side of the trickling stream.

"Chester," she called. "C-h-h-h-e-s-s-t-e-r-r!!!"

Just ahead was Possum Creek, where the natural spring joined other waters, which eventually spilled over Misty Falls, far beyond the family farm. Cassie, along with her brothers and sisters, had spent many hot afternoons diving off the boulder into the deep swimming hole. Over the years, they had made a game of finding the bottom of Possum Creek Swimming Hole, but they hadn't found it yet.

Cassie was starting to worry. Chester had never gone this far before. Perhaps he had crossed over the creek and onto someone else's property.

This was serious. Cassie thought it was time she got God involved in the search. She closed her eyes and tipped her head back toward the sky.

"Dear Lord, it's Cassie," she said. "Only You know where that crazy pony of mine is. Help me find him soon. It's getting dark, and Dad and I have to get him to the fairgrounds. Then I have to bake my cookies for the junior baking class exhibit. You already know about the blue ribbons and how important they are to me. Please Lord. This is really, really, really, really important. Thank You. In Jesus' name, Amen."

Cassie opened her eyes and started to retrace her steps, when she heard a loud *ker-thunk* further down-stream. It sounded like someone had thrown a bowling ball into the creek. *Ker-thunk!* There it went again.

Cassie strained to see what the matter could be, but a large bush sprouting wildly beside the creek was in her way. As fast as she could, she ducked through the undergrowth. What she saw next was sort of the size of a small hippopotamus, rolling itself happily in thick, gloppy mud along the side of the creek.

"Chester?" Cassie cried weakly. "Tell me it isn't you."

The muddy figure sat up, snorting, sputtering, and blinking two big round eyes at Cassie.

"Hhmmph," it said.

Cassie, You're a Winner!

"Oh, Chester, no. How could you?" she wailed.

Then a very muddy pony stood up and shook. Splats of mud flew everywhere, including all over Cassie.

Wiping mud out of her eye, Cassie peered longingly up toward the heavens and added a postscript to her prayer. "Maybe I didn't want to find Chester after all. I don't suppose it's too late to cancel my prayer request, is it, Lord?"

4

Now that she was reunited with her pony, Cassie had to fish him out of the mud. Then, another bath. Just thinking about this made her mad. Really mad.

She looked down at her shoes and legs, which were spattered with Chester's mud. Cassie huffed and puffed with frustration. She put her hands on her hips and stared at Chester.

As Chester blinked his muddy eyelids, she bellowed, "For Pete's sake! Just look at what you've done! You're spoiling everything. How could you do this to me?"

Chester blinked at her, as another glop of mud rolled off his back. He didn't seem to care at all. If Cassie hadn't felt so angry, she might have started laughing at such a funny sight.

She sighed again and said, "Come here, boy. Please don't make me come into that mud hole after you!"

Chester snorted. He seemed to be saying, "Why should I go with you? You didn't bring me any grain. Besides, I don't want another bath. This mud feels good."

Cassie hated feeling slimy and dirty. But there was no other way to get Chester. "Easy, boy," she whispered as she waded in up to her knees. She shivered with disgust as cool, icky mud oozed into her shoes and socks and between her toes.

Cassie kept her eyes on Chester. Just a few more steps, and she would be close enough to clip the lead rope onto his mud-covered halter.

"Easy, boy," she said, halfway holding her breath as she inched toward her pony. Chester sniffed at Cassie to make sure she didn't have a treat in her pocket.

Disappointed, he turned away from her, flipping his tail back and forth. As his tail swished, mud rained on Cassie's head.

Now that Chester had turned away from her, she had to wade further out in the muddy water, which was creeping up to her hips. "Come on, Chester. We'll go to the barn and get some grain."

Chester's ears perked, as though he might have recognized his favorite word. Grain was as tasty to Chester as chocolate was to Cassie.

Finally, she could almost reach Chester's halter. But then, just as she clipped the lead rope into the muddy ring under his chin, Cassie slipped. She let out a wailing "whoop," as she fell headfirst against Chester's muddy neck and side.

Cassie, You're a Winner!

Now with muddy hair, a muddy face, arms and clothes, Cassie felt like a chocolate-covered peanut. For a moment, she spewed and spit and wiped at her eyes. She could hardly see at all! But she was holding tight to Chester with the lead rope.

Glancing around, Cassie tried to figure out the best route back to dry ground. Then she had an idea. Gently clucking to Chester, she led him further up and into the creek, where they could both rinse off in clear water.

Chester stood motionless, while Cassie splashed his back with fresh water. After several minutes, she could see signs of his black and white spots under the mud. But the usually sparkling-clear creek was a cloudy mess by this time.

She shook her head and frowned at Chester. "It's going to take a gallon of shampoo to get you clean for the fair again. Come on, let's get home."

By the time the twosome found their way back to shore, both were sopping wet, and still very muddy. Walking across the south field had never seemed so endless. The soles of Cassie's soggy shoes seemed to attract more and more caked mud and grass as they went. Flies and mosquitoes joined their little party as they tromped through the pasture.

Finally, Cassie made it back to the barn, with Chester in tow. She put him in the cross ties, so that he wouldn't escape again and she placed a water hose, bucket, and bath supplies near him. The bath supplies consisted of shampoo, liquid fabric softener (which made a nice mane and tail conditioner), scrub brushes, sponges, and the last of the old towels that her mom had said were too worn out for the family to use anymore. She was determined to scrub Chester until his black and white coat glistened. The only thing she needed now was for Chester to cooperate.

First she turned on the water and rinsed herself off. Then she hosed down Chester. After three shampoos and lots of scrub-brushing, the white parts of his coat began to turn white again, not so orange from the mud. Still, Cassie wasn't satisfied. A blue-ribbon champion had to be really clean.

Chester began to paw the ground and snort. He was bored with this game and wanted to do something else.

"Too bad, boy," Cassie replied. "You asked for it. By the time I get through with you, you will be very sorry you ever rolled in that mud. And this time, you are going to stay clean."

After a total of five shampoos and six fabric softener rinses, Cassie was certain that her pony would be the cleanest show entry in her class, maybe in the whole fair. It was growing close to sunset by the time Cassie finished towel-drying Chester, and she placed him in a clean stall with his evening grain and hay. Chester munched pleasantly, nuzzling Cassie's arm as if to say,

"I'm so handsome and sweet. How could you be upset with me?"

"Yeah, right," said Cassie. "Don't look at me with those big brown eyes. If you ever do this to me again, Chester, I'll sell you to the circus."

Of course, Cassie would never sell Chester. But she wanted to sound serious, just in case Chester understood what a royal pain he had been.

Cassie's next challenge was going to be sneaking upstairs to the shower before Mom saw her. When she approached the back door of the house, she could hear her mother and sisters talking and pans clanging together. She was going to head around the house to the front door, when Greta, who was drying dishes, spied her out the window.

"Cassie! What happened to you?" she called. "You're a mess!" Mom and her big sisters Pat and Greta had caught her red-handed.

Her mom appeared in the doorway with her hands on her hips. "What on earth have you been doing, Cassidy Marie Holbrook?" she asked, sternly studying her daughter's wilted, muddy appearance.

Pat and Greta tried not to let Cassie see that they were laughing under their breath. But Cassie knew it, and she shot them a stern look of warning. "Don't even ask," she muttered.

Mom understood right away that this was not the time to go into details. "We went ahead without you.

Your plate's in the microwave."

"Thanks," Cassie said as she stepped inside the house. "I'm going upstairs to take a shower first."

"Good idea," said Mom. "But don't walk across the kitchen in those disgusting shoes, please!" Cassie nearly forgot. Being a farm family, the Holbrooks went through a lot of mud and dirt, but it was never allowed to be brought into the house—Mom made sure of that.

As she slipped off her shoes, Cassie recalled something very important. "Oh Mom, I'm baking my Snickerdoodles tonight, so I need the kitchen later."

"I remember, dear," said Mom cheerfully. "And you remember that your sisters are going to take their fair entries by the pavilion, and Aunt Mary and I are going to put our finishing touches on the quilts we're entering in the contest. We'll be in the living room if you need us, but we don't want to be disturbed unless it's absolutely necessary. Your father and the boys are working as fair parking attendants, and you agreed last week to watch your little cousin Petey for a while this evening."

Cassie stood staring at her mother in disbelief. "You're kidding! Mom, I have to bake my cookies. They have to be perfect. Please, can't you watch him?"

"No, I'm afraid not. We'll be too busy, and you know how active little Petey is. This would help so much, Cassie. It's only for an hour or two," said Mom.

Cassie, You're a Winner!

"Oh, and have you heard? Aunt Mary and Uncle Don are letting little Petey show a lamb at the fair tomorrow. Won't that be just adorable?"

"Adorable," muttered Cassie. She knew she was losing this argument even before she continued. "Mom, I can't be responsible for a six-year-old and bake a blue-ribbon batch of cookies at the same time."

"Fiddlesticks," said Mom, "Of course you can, and little Petey can watch. He's old enough to be a helper. You'll see, everything will be fine. Now hurry and get your shower, dear. Petey and Aunt Mary will be here any time now."

Cassie wanted to protest further, but her mother was already scurrying about, stacking baked goods on the table for her sisters to take to the fair.

Besides the "no-dirty-shoes-in-the-house" policy, there was another standing rule in the Holbrook family: "Always be ready to lend a helping hand." Cassie wished just for tonight that it wasn't her helping hand that was needed. Why couldn't Pat or Greta take care of Petey? It just didn't seem fair!

In the shower, Cassie let the warm water run over her face as she bathed and prayed.

"Lord, it's me again," she said. " Thanks for helping me find Chester, even though he was impossibly muddy. At least now he's ready to go to the fair tomorrow. But I need to ask another favor. Could you help me bake Snickerdoodles tonight? Ordinarily, it wouldn't be a problem. But my little cousin Petey makes Dennis the Menace look like an angel. Thanks God, and I'll try not to bother you again. Amen."

5

For once, Cassie didn't mind taking an extra-long shower. Scrubbing off the dried, caked mud was quite a challenge, but being mud-free and really clean helped put her in a better mood.

In fact, she considered staying in the bathroom all night. Cassie giggled to herself at the thought. Hiding was one way to avoid baby-sitting Petey. Of course, she would get pretty bored if she stayed there, but that was a small price to pay for peace and quiet—away from Petey! And she was pretty sure that God would understand.

Once the very warm water began to feel a bit chilly, she was ready to dry off and get dressed. *I must have used all the hot water,* Cassie said to herself as she turned the water off. *Well, I guess I need to get out now anyway. I need to start working on my blue-ribbon cookies!*

Cassie wrapped herself in a big, fluffy, yellow towel and scampered down the hall to her room. She could almost feel the time ticking by, and she was eager to start baking. If she hurried, maybe she could get the dough mixed up before energized, six-year-old Petey arrived.

She got dressed in her most comfy, knock-around clothes, and Opie tipped the door of her room open with his nose to invite himself in. He sat at her feet waiting to be petted. "I don't have time to love on you right now, Opie," she said, trying to comb the tangles out of her wet hair. "Come on, boy. Let's go downstairs and bake cookies."

Opie seemed to understand everything she said. He had been her closest companion since he came to live with the Holbrooks on Christmas Eve five years ago.

Still barefooted, Cassie scurried down the stairs with Opie close on her trail. In the kitchen, the counters were shiny and spotless—ready for Cassie to begin. She pulled out two mixing bowls, one large and one medium-sized, some mixing spoons, and a pan.

Cassie's stomach growled, and she felt a little weak. Then she realized why. In all the excitement of the first day of the fair and the muddy adventure with Chester, she had actually forgotten to eat! Thank goodness Mom had saved her dinner in the microwave.

"Mmm," said Cassie, opening the microwave door. She pulled out her plate of spaghetti. Her mom was such a good cook, and she had taught Cassie a lot about creating original recipes. Now, all she had learned was about to pay off! She smiled as she recalled her special recipe for Snickerdoodles, which tomorrow would win her the blue ribbon for sure.

As soon as Cassie's mouth wrapped around her loaded fork, Opie began to lick his lips and wag his tail. Finally, he stood up high on his hind legs and begged for a taste of Cassie's spaghetti.

Pointing in the direction of Opie's full dish of kibble, she said, "No, boy, you have your own food." She tried to ignore his whimpers as she finished her dinner. Then she put her fork and plate in the dishwasher, washed her hands, and began to work on her project.

Even though she knew her recipe by heart, she would take no risks. She clipped the recipe for Snickerdoodles into her mom's heart-shaped, tin recipe holder. Then she read each ingredient out loud as she placed everything on the counter beside the bowls.

"Butter," said Cassie, reading her recipe card. "And white, granulated sugar."

Before long, the ingredients were all laid out on the counter, except two—cream of tartar and cinnamon. Mom kept her spices high over the stove in the cabinet. Cassie couldn't reach up that far without some help.

In the broom closet, she got the stepladder and unfolded it. Climbing ever so carefully, Cassie stood on the tips of her toes at the top and reached for the cinnamon. It was in front, so it was easiest to get. The cream of tartar was way in the back, behind the nutmeg, ginger, and the peppercorns.

She could almost reach it, but not quite. Maybe if she moved the nutmeg just a little to the right....

All of a sudden, Opie began to bark. Cassie peered around, with her arm overhead, still stretching to reach the cream of tartar. Opie was standing on his hind legs, barking excitedly at the back door. He scrambled out of the kitchen to the front door for a closer look at the approaching guests. Cassie could hear his toe-nails clicking down the hallway on the hardwood flooring.

"It's Aunt Mary and little Petey, dear," announced Cassie's mother from the foyer. "I'm sending Petey into the kitchen. We're going to the other room now. Have fun!"

"Yeah, right," groaned Cassie. Every time she was around Petey, "fun" was not exactly how she would describe the experience. He was more like a bundle of disaster stuffed into a six-year-old body.

Just then, Petey burst into the kitchen with Opie excitedly at his feet. "Look what I brought!" he announced. He was holding a box that was almost as big as he was.

"Hi there," said Cassie, trying to sound cheerful. "What have you got?"

Petey set down the huge box and wiped his runny nose with his T-shirt. Then he sat down on the floor next to the box. "Help me set up my race car set," Petey demanded, his blond hair swinging as he gave the command.

He dumped all the contents of the box onto the floor. Out spilled tiny pieces of Jet-Set track, little Jet-Set racing cars, and batteries for the Jet-Set power modem. A bottle of Jet-Set Lubricating Oil rolled under the kitchen table. Petey didn't seem to notice. He was too busy setting up the racetrack.

"Oops, your bottle of oil rolled under the kitchen table, Petey. Why don't you get it before Opie does?" Cassie suggested.

"No!" said Petey. "I'm busy."

Cassie huffed and puffed. This was obviously going to be a very long night. And there was no use arguing with a six-year-old spoiled cousin. She got off the stepladder and crawled under the table. Opie was curiously sniffing at the bottle.

"Oh no you don't," said Cassie, grabbing it before he had a chance to put it in his mouth.

But Opie was distracted anyway. He had found a nearby piece of spaghetti noodle and sauce to gobble up. Cassie giggled. Mom had always said Opie was a mop on four legs. He would eat any little crumb or morsel that landed on the floor, so that was his job in the family.

Awkwardly crawling out from under the table, Cassie bumped her head on the corner of the table top. "Ouch!" she exclaimed, rubbing the top of her head.

She stood, dusted herself off, and placed the bottle of oil back in Petey's box.

Petey didn't say anything. He was snapping together pieces of racetrack. He made funny car sounds as he worked.

Cassie returned to the stepladder to get the cream of tartar. After a few minutes, her right arm was growing tired of trying to reach that little bottle. But her cookies couldn't win the blue ribbon without it. So she took a deep breath, stood higher on her tiptoes, and tried once more. Reaching, reaching, a little more...finally! She reached it!

Bringing the bottle out of the cabinet, Cassie's hand bumped the bottle of vanilla flavoring. Suddenly, like a slow-motion movie clip, all of the little bottles and cans of spice and flavorings came tumbling out of the cabinet. She ducked her head as the containers rained down on top of her.

With her hand tightly wrapped around the cream of tartar, Cassie squeezed her eyelids shut. She froze in place on the ladder, listening to the "thump, crash, pop, splat, clink" of the containers bouncing to the floor.

The clatter was followed by silence. Cassie opened one eye and peeked. Nothing seemed to be broken, but several caps had popped open. A mound of salt was pouring out of the box. Quite a lot of chili powder and oregano had dusted across the shiny linoleum.

Petey broke the silence. "Wow! You made a mess, Cassie. You'd better clean that up before your mom sees it." He shook his finger at Cassie for extra emphasis.

Cassie rolled her eyes and sighed. At least she had the cream of tartar for her cookies. She picked up the containers and returned them to the spice cabinet over the stove.

Meanwhile, Petey drew designs in the dusting of ingredients. Then he spelled his name in the salt. "P-E-T-E-Y. Petey!" he exclaimed proudly.

Opie sniffed at the mix of spilled powders. He snorted and sneezed. "Get away from there, Opie," said Cassie, closing the cabinet door over the stove. "I've got enough to clean up, and I don't need you making an even bigger mess."

Petey drove his racing cars through the grainy dust. He made noises for the imaginary motors of his cars.

Cassie quickly folded the ladder and returned it to the closet. Next, she got the broom and shooed Opie away from the spills. Sweeping up hundreds of tiny little particles was much harder than Cassie expected, but she managed to clean up the spills.

"You forgot to get that red powder over there," said Petey, pointing under a nearby chair.

Cassie sighed. "Thanks," she said. "You're a big help."

"I like to help," said Petey with a confident grin

spread across his face. Cassie noticed that Petey's jeans were covered in salt, chili powder, and oregano.

"Oh, Petey, let's go outside and dust you off."

"I don't want to go outside. I have to drive my race cars. It's the Indy 500, and I'm going to win."

Cassie didn't want to argue. She took him by the arm and coaxed him onto his feet. "The Indy 500 can wait. Come on, right now!"

"Cassie, how come you're so bossy?" said Petey, complaining all the way outside.

"It will only take a minute," said Cassie. "I have cookies to bake. Now just cooperate."

"Co-op-er-what?" said Petey, wiping his nose on his T-shirt.

"Never mind," said Cassie, dusting off his knees. "That's better. Now you can get back to the Indy 500."

As Cassie and Petey joined Opie back in the kitchen, Petey said, "I'm hungry. Do you have any pickles?"

"Pickles?" Cassie asked. "You don't like pickles."

"I do now," said Petey. "Got any? I like the sour ones."

"You mean dill pickles," said Cassie, searching in the refrigerator. "Here they are. Are you sure you want a pickle?"

"I want two," said Petey. Cassie set the open jar onto the counter and got a plate to hold Petey's pickles.

"Crunch!" He bit into one. Even though his eyes watered a little bit, he seemed to like the taste.

Cassie was surprised because Petey didn't even like

most regular foods. She shrugged and went on with her work.

Now that all the cookie dough ingredients were on the counter, Cassie got the sifter and the mixer.

"Stop doing that and play cars with me," said Petey.

"Maybe later," said Cassie. "I'm really busy with my baking, and my cookies have to be just perfect. They're going to the fair tomorrow morning. You can play with your cars by yourself."

"No!" exclaimed Petey. He shook his head so hard, that his long, blond hair shook. "Petey wants you to play cars—now!"

"Calm down," said Cassie, trying to be patient. "Tell you what. I'll play cars with you, after the dough is made. While the dough is chilling in the freezer, I will play cars with you. First, I need you to be my helper."

"Can I eat some?" asked Petey, munching his pickle. Cassie couldn't imagine eating Snickerdoodles right after dill pickles. Petey was just asking for a stomachache.

"Well," said Cassie, stalling. "If you will be a good helper, you may taste the cookie dough when we're finished. Deal?"

Petey grinned. "Deal," he said, quickly adding, "I like cookie dough. Sometimes Mommy lets me eat a glop of dough before she cooks the cookies."

"A glop?" laughed Cassie. "Well, you'd better wash your hands first."

"I don't want to wash my hands," said Petey.

"They're clean enough."

"Let me see," said Cassie. Petey held out his hands for Cassie's inspection. Opie's fur, pickle juice, and little-boy dirt covered Petey's hands. They were filthy.

"Okay, let's wash," said Cassie. She practically had to drag him to the sink to wash his hands. She didn't even care that Petey was squawking about it. He would be squeaky clean before getting anywhere near her Snickerdoodles. Nothing was going to ruin this perfect, blue-ribbon batch of cookies.

6

Cassie took a deep breath to help her get focused again. She set the oven for 400 degrees, just like she had done a hundred times before.

"Finally, we're ready to start the prize-winning Snickerdoodles!" exclaimed Cassie.

"Snickerdoodles, Snickerdoodles," repeated Petey. Cassie chuckled. Even Petey could say the word, so why couldn't Iggy?

At the kitchen counter, she looked over the ingredients before her— flour, sugar, cinnamon, salt, baking soda, eggs, pure butter, and her secret ingredients, buttermilk, and cream of tartar.

With Mom's recipe card holder in front of her, Cassie read her own personal, original recipe. This batch of cookies was going to be perfect.

Cassie's Snickerdoodles
Deluxe

With a mixer, cream:

1 cup real butter
1½ cups sugar
2 eggs
1 tablespoon buttermilk

Sift and add to butter mixture:

2¾ cups sifted flour
2 teaspoons cream of tartar
1 teaspoon baking soda
½ teaspoon salt
1½ teaspoons cinnamon

Chill dough. Drop by spoonfuls 2 inches apart on greased baking sheet. Bake at 400 degrees for 8-10 minutes. Makes 5 dozen snickerdoodles.

Petey and Cassie set to work double-sifting the flour. Cassie knew that double-sifting the flour would make the cookies light and fluffy.

"Let me do it by myself," said Petey. "I wanna shift the flour."

"Sift, not shift," said Cassie. "Here, you can try all by yourself. No, not over the floor, in the mixing bowl, for Pete's sake. That's better."

"For Petey's sake," said Petey as he sifted wildly.

After the dry ingredients were sifted together into one of the mixing bowls, Cassie creamed the butter with the mixer. Next she added sugar, then eggs.

Petey grabbed an egg and threw it into the bowl. The egg broke. Pieces of eggshell floated on top of the mixture. Cassie turned off the electric mixer.

"No, Petey!" she said. "Look what you did." She fished out the broken eggshell pieces.

Petey stuck his finger into the bowl and tasted the batter. "Mmm, can I have some cookies now?"

"They aren't done yet," said Cassie. "Look, I have an idea. While I finish this, why don't you grease the cookie pan for me, so the cookies won't stick when we bake them? There's the shortening. Just rub it very lightly over the pan. Okay?"

"Oh boy," said Petey. "Don't help me, Cassie. I know how."

"Good," said Cassie, trying to relax a little. Maybe Petey was going to be helpful after all. She combined the flour mixture with the butter, sugar, and egg mixture. Now her blue-ribbon cookie dough was really on its way.

Opie ran to Cassie's feet, tapped her ankle with his wet nose, and walked to the door. It was his signal that he needed to go outside.

Cassie stopped the mixer. She glanced at Petey, who had gotten bored and was playing with his cars. "I'll be right back," she said and took Opie outside.

Like always, Opie liked to sniff around to find just the right spot. "Hurry up, Opie," scolded Cassie. "I need to get back to my cookies."

Opie finished, and the two headed back inside.

When Cassie returned to the kitchen, Petey was mixing the dough in the bowl. He was doing a very good job. "Wow," said Cassie, "You are a good helper, Petey."

"I like to help," said Petey, beaming. Cassie was sure that this dough truly did seem even lighter and creamier than all the other times she had baked Snickerdoodles for her family.

Only one step remained before Cassie could bake her cookies. The dough would need to chill in the freezer for about fifteen minutes to become stiff, so that they would bake properly. Cassie proudly covered her prize dough with plastic wrap. But before she could place the dough into the freezer, Petey began to holler.

"I want a taste," he announced. "You promised I could have a glop of cookie dough."

Cassie looked at him and sighed. He was all dusty with flour and sticky with egg, butter, and sugar on his hands. She couldn't help smiling as she uncovered the dough and spooned some out for Petey. She handed him the spoon. Cassie covered the dough again and placed it inside the freezer.

Petey admired the shiny ball of dough. "I helped make Snickerdoodles," he sang. "Now I get to lick the Snickerdoodle spoon! Oh boy!"

Amused, Cassie watched as Petey's eyes grew wide with delight. He held the spoon before his open mouth. His loose front tooth wiggled against his pink tongue that stuck out as far as it could. Opie cocked his head to one side and eyed Petey's spoon with great interest. He salivated and wagged his tail hopefully, but Petey did not intend to share his cookie dough. Licking a big swirl of dough off the side of the spoon, Petey smacked his lips together. After a moment or two, the dough erupted from his mouth in a series of spitting and spewing. The cookie dough tumbled out of his mouth and onto the kitchen floor.

"Stop that!" cried Cassie. "For Pete's sake, what's the matter?"

Coughing and sputtering, Petey wiped his tongue on the front of his T-shirt.

"This tastes terrible! Icky!"

Cassie, You're a Winner!

Opie sniffed at the cookie dough that Petey had spit onto the floor. But just as the dog was about to clean it up with his tongue, he heard a noise outside. Suddenly Opie forgot all about Petey's rejected cookie dough and began running merrily in circles around the kitchen. Mom and Aunt Mary entered the kitchen as Pat and Greta came in the back door. Opie lay down and enjoyed a belly rub from Pat, and then Greta.

Aunt Mary took one look at Petey and began to laugh. "What on earth is on your T-shirt?" she asked, pointing to the smears of cookie dough.

"Cassie made me eat icky cookie dough! It tastes awful, Mommy, not like your cookie dough. I want to go home now!" cried Petey.

"What?" asked Cassie. She was totally confused. This was the best cookie dough ever. *Why was Petey behaving this way?* she wondered.

"What did you do to him, Cassie?" asked Aunt Mary, consoling her little son.

"Nothing. I…" sputtered Cassie.

She couldn't think. She was suddenly stunned, confused, and very, very tired. First Chester, now Petey. Everything today seemed totally out of control.

Aunt Mary picked up Petey. "There, there, Petey, Mommy's here," she said in a sickening, sweet way. "Cassie, honey, don't worry. It's past his bedtime. I'm sure he's just tired. Now is there anything I need to know before I take him home?"

Cassie just stood there motionless. Finally, she answered. "I guess he ate Snickerdoodle dough after he ate pickles. He probably has a tummy ache."

Aunt Mary laughed, said goodnight, and carried Petey out to the van. They left before Cassie realized that Petey had left his Jet-Set racing stuff all over the floor. Cassie and her mom picked it all up and put the pieces back into the box.

"We'll return the racing set to him tomorrow," said Mom. "Now, why don't you tell me what happened."

Cassie shrugged her shoulders. "I don't know. We were just making Snickerdoodles. Petey wanted to taste them, so I gave him a spoonful to taste. For some reason, he didn't like it. I guess the sweet taste wasn't good after eating dill pickles."

"Dill pickles?" asked Mom. "I'm surprised Petey would eat sour pickles."

"That's what I thought," said Cassie. "Oh well. I'm sorry the kitchen is such a mess, Mom. I'll clean it up now."

"I'll help you, dear," said Mom. "It's getting quite late."

After Opie enjoyed a long tummy rubbing, he remembered that he still had a snack to gobble up— Petey's rejected spoonful of cookie dough. Cassie was just getting ready to wipe it up with a paper towel, when Opie dove into the dough nose first. Just as quickly as Opie had begun to lick it, though, he began pawing strangely at his mouth. Then he began drinking from his water bowl. He drank and drank and drank, without stopping. Finally, all of his water was gone. Then, tucking his tail between his legs, Opie ran out of the kitchen to his favorite hiding spot under the sofa in the living room.

"How strange," Cassie thought. Maybe Opie didn't like the cinnamon flavor.

Cassie went to the freezer and examined her dough. Sure enough, it was the most beautiful, shiniest dough she had ever made. She began spooning out the shiny chilled dough into little balls and placing them on the greased cookie sheet. Next, she slid her pan of cookies into the hot oven to bake. She set the timer for eight minutes. Then she licked a little dough off her index finger. Right away, the familiar sweet, buttery cinnamon flavor greeted her taste buds, and she smiled with satisfaction.

"Mmmm," said Cassie to her mother. But then, something strange began to happen. Her tongue began to tingle and sting. "This is...gross!" Cassie tried helplessly to spit out the vile taste into the sink. "Oh, Mom, what's wrong with my blue-ribbon cookies?"

She could have cried buckets of tears. But she had to figure out why her cookie dough tasted so incredibly awful. Nothing like this had ever happened before!

"Let's just be calm," said Mom. "Tell me step-by-step how you made the cookies."

Cassie wiped her eyes, which were burning from the bitter taste in her mouth. But she refused to give in to tears. She told Mom about Petey wanting to play race cars, and how the only way she could bake her cookies was to let him help her. She named each ingredient aloud as she placed it back into the cabinets.

"Flour, sugar, baking soda, salt, lubricating oil..."

"Lubricating oil?" asked Mom, confused. "Lubricating oil!" shouted Cassie. "Oh, this goes with Petey's race car set. Mom, you don't suppose he put Jet-Set Lubricating Oil in my blue-ribbon Snickerdoodles, do you?"

Mom looked amused. But this wasn't funny. She picked up another ingredient off the counter. "Cassie, does your recipe call for a whole jar of cream of tartar?"

"For Pete's sake!" yelled Cassie. Downhearted, Cassie sat cross-legged on the floor in front of the oven door. She peered into the window at her cookies. She could see that the cookies were rising quite nicely. New hope began to spring from her heart. She squeezed her eyes shut so tightly that they hurt.

"Dear Jesus," she prayed fervently, "I have believed that You are God's Son ever since I can remember. You're the one who went around doing miracles in the Bible. You healed people, turned a little boy's fish and bread into a feast for thousands, and all kinds of neat stuff. This is just one little pan of cookies. No

Cassie, You're a Winner!

matter what Petey did to my Snickerdoodles, You can make them turn out beautiful and delicious. I just know You can. And I believe You will. I'm counting on You, Lord. Thank you! Amen."

Before Cassie even opened her eyes, she breathed a great big breath and held it. Ever so slowly, she opened one eye, then the other. She peeked into the oven window, ready to watch the mighty miracle unfold.

Perhaps the smoke that was starting to rise from around the edges of the cookie pan was the result of God's holy touch. Strange, gloppy bubbles formed and popped on the surface of each Snickerdoodle. Perhaps that was how God was getting rid of Petey's ingredients, which didn't belong in her cookies.

"Thank you, God! You did hear my prayers!" whispered Cassie excitedly. "And, you're answering!" Her lips curled into a tired but victorious smile.

Cassie's mother bent over her daughter and softly touched her shoulders. "Dear, you really should get to bed. You have a busy day tomorrow. Why don't you run upstairs and get into your pajamas? I'll throw out the cookies, and you make another batch in the morning."

"Oh no, Mom!" cried Cassie. "Don't throw them out. These are going to be perfect."

"What?" Mom seemed doubtful. "Are you sure?"

"I'm very sure," said Cassie peacefully. "I've prayed over these cookies. With God's help, these

Snickerdoodles will taste even better than usual. You just wait and see. The judges will love them! Just have a little faith, Mom!"

Cassie could almost see question marks in her mom's dark, loving eyes. But why shouldn't she be as confident as Cassie felt? After all, she was a veteran Sunday School teacher. Since Cassie was old enough to walk and talk, Mom had preached about trusting God, believing in His healing touch, and having something called faith in Him.

Mom always said that having faith in God was kind of like believing that the wind was blowing, even though wind is invisible.

Many times, through the years, Mother would tell Cassie, "Even though you can't see the wind blowing, you know it is there. You can see the tree branches swaying. We can't see God with our eyes, but we know He is there, because we see the results of His work all around us. Trust Him, Cassie. Have faith that He will help you."

It was true. Cassie believed all of her mom's words. Her mom knew the Bible better than anyone Cassie had ever known. Funny, now that Cassie was counting on God, Mom seemed doubtful. Cassie was sure she would never understand adults.

"Well," said Mom finally, as she looked into the smoky oven, "if it means that much to you. But I want you to go on to bed now. I promise to take out your cookies right on time and store them for you. Perhaps things will be clearer to you in the morning."

Mom had that "don't argue with me" look on her face. So Cassie just sighed and slowly went up to bed. By the time she reached the landing at the top of the stairs, her body felt as limp as an old, stretched-out rubber band.

Cassie didn't even notice Pat and Greta giggling about the cookie smoke drifting upstairs from the kitchen. She didn't care that she wasn't in her pajamas.

The sheets on her bed had never felt softer, and Cassie fell asleep as soon as her head nestled into the pillow. That night, she had the most wonderful dream....

She was at the show arena at Misty Falls Fairgrounds, where the horse judging was about to begin. Everyone competing simply glittered in their show costumes. There was J.J., already mounted on Gracie, looking like a beautiful princess. The wonderful smell of freshly popped corn was wafting in the air.

Colors in Cassie's dream seemed brighter and bolder than colors in real-life. Yellow sunshine had never been so buttery golden before. Green grass had never been so velvety green. And most importantly, blue ribbons had never been so royally blue.

And Chester was absolutely gorgeous! His coat couldn't have been shinier if it had been slicked down in oil. And for some strange reason, Chester was looking mighty and muscular. His usual pot belly was gone! In its place was a row of sleek, rippling muscles. Cassie gasped with joy as she admired her beautiful, simply perfect pony.

Gallantly, proudly, Cassie carried her head extra high as she led Chester out of the show barn toward the waiting arena. Just as she had hoped, the crowds of onlookers in the stands went wild with applause. Their cheering grew louder as Cassie and Chester walked nearer. Chester nickered and shook his flashy mane at his admirers. Cassie flashed a smile toward the stands. The fans roared with fresh applause.

A gentle breeze lightly whipped wisps of her light auburn hair against her eyelashes as she walked toward the arena. She could feel her heartbeat speed up as she strode confidently to the gate of the arena. As Cassie mounted Chester's back and gathered up the reins, a hush fell over the waiting crowd.

Indeed, Chester stole every heart in the crowd with his splendid performance. He pranced. He danced. He trotted. He cantered. He whoa-ed. And he did it all with grace and dignity. All Cassie had to do was enjoy the ride. The judges beamed as they announced the winner of the competition into the loud speaker: "First place goes to Cassie Holbrook and the most amazing pony we have ever seen, Chester."

As the announcement was made, a sea of applause met her ears. Cassie looked around and saw J.J. cheering excitedly for her. Then Cassie leaned over Chester's neck to shake the judges' hands. It was the proudest moment of Cassie's life!

Still sitting on Chester's back, she fell forward to tightly hug Chester. "We did it, boy! We won the blue ribbon."

Cassie, You're a Winner!

Just then, Iggy ran into the arena and started taking pictures of Cassie and Chester and their beautiful blue ribbon with his camera. "Say 'cheese dip', Cassie. You're the star of the show!"

"Cheese dip," *said Cassie, shaking with excitement. She couldn't wait to see her picture in the newspaper!*

A voice that seemed strangely far away called out her name. "Cassie, Cassie, wake up! You're having a nightmare."

"Cheese dip," said Cassie. Then she felt a pair of hands on her shoulders, shaking her.

"Wake up!" The voice was strong and loud. Cassie opened her eyes and saw her sister Greta standing over her in the moon shadows. "Greta! I didn't know you were here! Isn't it wonderful? I won!"

But somehow or another, the sunshine, the arena and all the crowds, contestants, and horses had disappeared. Cassie suddenly found herself twisted in the covers near the foot of her bed, muttering "Cheese dip."

That's funny, she thought. *Iggy was just here with his camera a minute ago.* "Where did everybody go?"

Greta giggled. "I don't know what you were dreaming about, Little Sis, but it must have been quite a dream."

"Chester won the blue ribbon," said Cassie. "It was so cool, Greta."

"Okay, congratulations," said Greta, yawning. "Just keep your dreaming to yourself for the rest of the night, please. I could hear you in my room way across the hall!"

As soon as Greta had gone back to her room and closed her door, Cassie slipped out of bed. In nothing but her T-shirt and pajama boxer shorts, she quietly made her way downstairs. Something wet touched the back of her ankle as she started down the stairs.

She gasped and looked behind her. Two beady eyes stared at her in the semi-darkness. "Opie! Stop that! Why do you always have to touch me with your cold, wet nose? That's disgusting."

Opie wagged his tail as Cassie sighed and bent down to scratch the backs of his ears. "Oh, alright," she said. "You can come with me."

Now that he had formally been invited, Opie trotted down the stairs ahead of Cassie. At the back door, Cassie slipped on her old barn shoes and made her way across the drive to the barn. Opie ran ahead to see if he could sneak up on the cat or get into some other delightful mischief. Cassie flipped on the lights in the barn and blinked until her eyes adjusted to the brightness. Then she peered into Chester's stall.

There was her trusty steed, still shining from the extensive bath he received earlier. He had rolled in the fresh wood shavings, but his coat would brush out nicely in the morning. Cassie smiled dreamily as Chester yawned. "I know it's late," said Cassie, "but I just couldn't wait to tell you something, Chester."

Cassie, You're a Winner!

Cassie opened the door and walked into his stall. She hugged him around his soft, warm neck. Chester nickered softly and leaned into Cassie's arms for a bit more loving. "We won, Chester," she whispered. "I know now it was just a dream, but tomorrow, my dream will come true. I just know it. Good night, boy. I'll see you in the morning."

Cassie closed the stall door and looked around for Opie. "Opie, you silly dog, where are you?" Opie was stealing a bite of kibble out of the cat's food dish. "I should have known you were eating. Come on, we've got to get these barn lights turned off and get back to bed."

Suddenly, Opie barked and perked his ears. A mouse darted across the barn floor, and nearly scared Cassie to pieces. "Shh," she said to Opie. "Will you be quiet? It's just a little mouse. Come on, you're going to wake up the whole family!"

On his short little legs, Opie trotted quickly out of the barn, ran to the back door, and waited to be let in.

Cassie slipped out of her shoes and through the kitchen. She could still smell her fresh Snickerdoodles. She smiled, thinking about the heavenly fragrance and her two blue ribbons she would claim tomorrow.

Back up the stairs Cassie and Opie went. This time, Opie hopped into bed with Cassie and curled up against her legs.

7

Awaking with a start, Cassie glanced at her clock. It was already 7:00 A.M. The dawning of her blue-ribbon day had finally arrived!

Her western outfit that she would wear in the horse show was hanging neatly on a hook in her closet. Dressing quickly, she admired herself in the full-length mirror. Perfect.

She hurried to the kitchen for orange juice and a final look at her Snickerdoodles. Mother had beautifully arranged the cookies on a plate and covered them with pink plastic wrap. They were a lovely golden brown. Snickerdoodles touched by the Lord would certainly win first prize, she thought happily.

Her dad stumbled into the kitchen wearing denim jeans and a brand new Misty Falls Fair T-shirt. He yawned and slowly sipped on his big mug of steaming coffee.

"Good morning, Munchkin," he said, pausing to kiss the top of her head. He scratched his own head, where it looked like birds had made a nest overnight. His black and silver hair was sticking out in all directions, with a pressed-down balding spot in the middle.

"Dad, your hair," Cassie giggled. "Want me to run up and get your comb?"

"Nah," said Dad. "It's going to be under a baseball cap all day, anyhow. I hear you had a right interesting time of it last night. Sorry I wasn't here to help you load up old Chester."

Alarmed, Cassie looked wide-eyed into her father's own deep blue eyes. "Oh Dad, I forgot all about getting Chester to the fairgrounds. Will you help me this morning?"

"Why, sure I will," he said, in his easy-going manner. "Almost ready."

"Good morning, Sunshine," said Mom, as she entered the kitchen, wrapped in her mint green terrycloth robe. "Did you sleep well, Cassie? Oh, I see you found your Snickerdoodles. Now are you certain that you want to take them to the fair?"

Cassie was about to reply, but Dad spoke first. "But Honey, I thought you said those cookies weren't fit for a dog." Cassie's eyes grew wide.

Mom smacked Dad's arm. "Joe Holbrook!" she scolded. "I said no such thing. I merely said that I was worried they wouldn't taste as good as usual, because Petey added extra ingredients."

Cassie, You're a Winner!

It was a good thing that Cassie was in such a good mood. She wasn't about to let Mom's doubts cloud her thinking. "Oh ye of little faith. Isn't that what you always tell us kids, Mom? Petey or no Petey, I'm going to win that blue ribbon today. I have faith!"

"But Cassie," Mom began gently.

Dad interrupted. "That's the spirit," he said, giving Cassie a big bear hug. "That's my Cassie. What you've got there is the most handsome plate of cookies that ever came out of the Holbrook kitchen. Yep, it's a winner alright."

That's what she liked about her father. He always had something positive to say, and it always came from his heart. Why couldn't Mom be more like that?

"Would you like a cookie, Dad?" asked Cassie. "There are plenty."

Dad looked at Mom. His face turned a little red. "Uh, that's alright, Munchkin," he said. "It's a little early in the day to eat cookies. Besides, we'd better get old Chester and Maggie loaded in the trailer. Come on, let's go."

"Okay," said Cassie. "I'll get Chester and meet you at the trailer."

"Alright, Munchkin," he said with a wink. He and Cassie each kissed Mom, who promised to be ready to leave in twenty minutes. Dad went to the old barn to fetch his prize heifer, Maggie, and Cassie walked toward the new barn to prepare Chester for his big day at the fair.

Adventures in Misty Falls

Walking into a world of sunshine and blue skies felt great. On her way to the barn, Cassie breathed in the sweet country air that smelled of pine trees and morning dew.

Aside from sore muscles from her adventure with Chester yesterday, Cassie felt wonderful. She was going to show her pony this morning, then her cookies this afternoon. It really felt like a double-winner day!

Within a few minutes, Cassie's cookies were stored on the front seat of the truck. Dad helped Cassie load Chester and his heifer in the trailer. After the last of the horse tack was loaded, Cassie and her family were off to the fair.

Dad and Cassie dropped off Mom and Greta at the food exhibit hall. "We'll deliver your cookies to the juniors exhibit. Then we'll come down for your horse show," said Greta, looking around anxiously. Cassie knew that she was looking for her high school friends. Then they swapped smiles. "Go for it, Sis."

"Okay, thanks," called Cassie, waving to her sister.

Dad quickly unloaded Chester and the tack and continued on to the cattle barn with his heifer. "I'll see you in a while, Munchkin. Have a good day," he called as he pulled away.

Cassie was glad to be on her own with Chester. When they located his stall, he seemed to be glad to be next door to Gracie, his companion from the times J.J. and Cassie went trail riding together. Gracie and

Cassie, You're a Winner!

Chester rubbed noses over the wall and swished their tails happily. Cassie put down a flake of hay for Chester's breakfast and a scoop of grain in his bucket. She brought fresh water for him. Chester nuzzled Cassie's arm gratefully as he munched his grain. Cassie smiled happily as she thought of winning the show with her beloved Chester.

While he finished his feeding, Cassie saddled him up. Then she slipped on a brand new, forest green vest that Mom and Pat had made for her. It looked very handsome with her tan jeans and hat and her polished, dark brown riding boots.

Cassie rubbed down Chester's head, neck, legs, and hind quarters with baby oil to give his coat extra shine. She didn't even notice J.J. until she popped her head over the stall and said, "Boo!"

J.J. opened the stall door and joined Cassie and Chester. She looked beautiful in her blue and red sparkling sequined jacket and her sleek, black accessories. Cassie thought she and Gracie looked professional enough to be in *International Equine Magazine*.

"Cassie, I'm so excited for you! This is your very first horse show. I remember how special my first show was. Are you nervous?" asked J.J.

Cassie blinked. "Huh? Oh yeah. I guess my mind has been on those silly cookies. I forgot to be nervous."

J.J. giggled. "That's a good sign! You will do great, and so will Chester."

Before the girls could really even start their usual chattering and giggling, they heard the announcement over the loud speaker. "Ladies and gentlemen, welcome to our Junior Classes Equine Horse Show. We will begin in five minutes."

In a flash, J.J. took Gracie by the halter and led her out of her stall. "Gotta go, Cass! I'm in the first class. We warmed up early this morning. When do you show?"

"Third class," said Cassie. "Chester and I will come out and watch you!"

"Wish me luck," said J.J. as she mounted Gracie and rode her out of the barn.

Cassie followed with Chester. She led him beside the fence to watch J.J.'s performance. As always, J.J. made showing horses look so effortless. She cantered around the outside arena with such ease. No one else in the class displayed as much horsemanship and grace as J.J. and her mare. Cassie sighed dreamily.

"It will be our turn soon," Cassie whispered to Chester.

She didn't have to wait long to find out that J.J. was awarded the blue ribbon, just as Cassie had expected. J.J. and Gracie took a victory walk around the ring, while the satin blue ribbon fluttered in the breeze. Applause swelled from the stands.

"Way to go, J.J.!" Cassie shouted. J.J. responded with a wink as she passed by at a quick trot.

Cassie, You're a Winner!

As the announcer called for Class 2 to begin, Cassie decided to warm up Chester for his show. Outside the show arena, she mounted her pony and made a clucking sound to make him go.

But instead of walking forward, Chester just stood there, blinking in the sunlight. She clucked to him again. "Let's go, boy," she urged.

Still, Chester would not move. He curled his neck around and gave Cassie a look that seemed to say, "Excuse me. I'm enjoying the morning sunshine and do not wish to be disturbed."

Cassie squeezed Chester's sides firmly with her leg muscles. Once again, she clucked to him, signaling that she wanted him to "come up," or "walk forward." Chester just snorted casually.

"Chester, I said 'go'!" Cassie gave Chester a swift kick. Chester stamped his right foot, laid his ears back, and planted his feet squarely, refusing to move.

Now Cassie was getting mad. She remembered what J.J. had taught her back in the spring about letting the horse know who is in control. Cassie was determined to show him who was in control. She was!

"Chester, you are the most stubborn creature on this earth. Now, let's go!" With that, Cassie kicked Chester's sides with all the strength she could muster. Chester heaved a great sigh and looked rather bored.

Just then, the car-racing event across the fairgrounds began with a single gunshot fired in the air.

Though nothing else had worked, the loud gunshot got Chester's attention.

All of a sudden, Chester threw back his head, vaulted onto his hind legs, and plunged forward at a full gallop. Cassie unsteadily hung on for dear life. With one hand firmly gripping the saddle horn and the reins in the other hand, Cassie tried her best to steer Chester through the crowds and between fair buildings, rides, and tents.

"Whoa, boy! Whoa!" yelled Cassie, as her hat flew off into Chester's dust. "Please stop!" Chester whinnied loudly in protest and kept running.

All of the horses, riders, and spectators in the stands had stopped paying attention to what was going on in the riding arena. They were busy watching the entertaining antics of Cassie and Chester. In fact, so was everyone in Chester's path! And Cassie wasn't sure, but she thought she caught a glimpse of Iggy's red hair in the crowd near the pavilions. But Chester didn't slow down long enough for Cassie to be sure it was Iggy or to call out for help.

Cassie just wanted to get off Chester and onto solid ground. In fact, she was quite certain that she did not really want to be in this horse show after all. Or any other horse show. Ever.

8

Chester was the gentlest pony Cassie knew, but he was also the most stubborn equine on the planet. It didn't surprise Cassie when Chester ran them both back to the barn as fast as he could get there. And Cassie no longer felt like fighting him for control.

As soon as Chester reached his stall, he halted. He stood breathless in front of the big barn fan, cooling down. Shakily, Cassie descended from the saddle. Her hair was a big auburn mess, and her white shirt was sort of orange-brown from all the dust Chester had stirred up. Just then, Chester nuzzled Cassie's face as if to say, "I'm sorry." Then he snorted to clear the dust from his nostrils and just happened to spray all over her.

Cassie wiped her face with the sleeve of her newly ruined western show shirt. Instead of feeling angry at Chester, she was relieved to be on solid ground again.

"What a pair we are, Chester. Come on," she said, blinking dust out of her eyes. Her heart was pumping double-time. Her quivering legs felt mushy as she led him into his stall and took off his saddle. There was no way that Cassie was going to show him or any horse after that frightening episode.

Chester let her remove his bridle. Happy to be free of the bit in his mouth, he nosed into his grain bucket for leftovers. As she brushed him, Greta sped into the barn.

"Cassie, where are you? Are you alright?" she asked frantically. Cassie liked both her sisters. But she especially felt fond of Greta, who was going to be a senior in high school soon.

"Here I am, and we're fine," said Cassie, trying to sound cheerful. She didn't want anyone, even Greta, to know how frightened she had been.

Greta came into the stall. "Chester, you bad boy!" Then she realized Cassie was putting away the tack. "Oh Cass, you're not quitting, are you?"

Cassie smiled bravely, shrugged her shoulders and tried to think of a good response. "Oh, Chester just isn't a show horse, but don't worry, I'm fine. Let's go out and cheer for J.J., okay? She has another show coming up."

Still shaking from the experience, Cassie unsteadily went out of the stall and closed the gate securely. Chester looked at her and nickered lowly. Poor Chester must have been scared, too, scared of that gunshot at the racing event.

Cassie, You're a Winner!

As they strolled toward the stands, Cassie noticed several people were whispering to each other and pointing at her. A heavy wave of embarrassment washed over her. She tried to act like she didn't care.

"Look," said Greta. No sooner had Greta spoken, Cassie spotted Aunt Mary and Petey in the distance. They were unloading Petey's lamb at the sheep barn on the crest of the hill beyond the performance ring.

Aunt Mary waved wildly to her nieces. "Yoo hoo! Cassie, help us!" she called.

"Oh great, what now?" muttered Cassie. But in a way, she was glad to get away from the horse arena for a while. "Greta, you go ahead. I'll go see what they want."

"Okay. Are you sure you're alright?"

Cassie mustered a smile.

"Well," said Greta, smoothing her little sister's hair, "if you're not going to show your horse, I'll meet you later in the food pavilion."

"See you later," Cassie called, still trying to sound more cheerful than she felt. Inside she was unbearably disappointed in herself.

As Cassie approached, Aunt Mary was chattering a mile a minute. It was something about an emergency at the hospital where she worked and how she had to get there right away. And since Petey just loved being with Cassie, Aunt Mary asked if she would stay with him and help him get the lamb ready to show.

Cassie sighed. "Why not?" she said. Then silently, she thought, *Why not, indeed!* She couldn't help thinking what a mess Petey made of her cookies last night.

Petey's mouth was covered with peanut butter crackers. "Look Cassie, this is my lamb, Sweet Pea. Isn't she pretty?"

"Baaa," said Sweet Pea.

"I'll be back soon," said Aunt Mary. "But if I don't make it back for Petey's show, it's the first class. Here's the camera. Take pictures for me, will you?" Aunt Mary plopped the camera into Cassie's hands. Then she studied Cassie more closely. "Are you alright, dear? You don't look well."

Cassie smiled weakly, looking down at peanut buttery Petey. "Oh, I'm fine. Just fine."

Petey grinned. "Bye Mom. Me and Cassie will take care of Sweet Pea."

Off went Aunt Mary. Now it was just Cassie, Petey, and Sweet Pea, lost in a Misty Falls Fair nightmare.

As soon as Aunt Mary disappeared in her van, Petey turned to Cassie and licked peanut butter off his sticky lips. Then he pronounced, "You don't really have to help me. I'm old enough to take care of Sweet Pea myself."

Cassie sighed and rolled her eyes. "Oh no you don't, Petey. Your mom told me I am in charge. Don't argue, because I am not in the mood."

With that, Cassie took Petey by the hand and Sweet

Cassie, You're a Winner!

Pea by the leash, and dragged them into the barn.

With Petey protesting all the way and Sweet Pea bellowing happily, the three of them walked past the other sheep and owners who were preparing for their show events. "Cassie, how come you're so bossy?"

Cassie looked at her little cousin with a frown. "Because I am the boss," she said firmly.

Petey stared at her with his peanut-butter-and-cracker mouth hanging open. With his eyes wide, he swallowed hard, and asked, "Ya wanna help me brush out Sweet Pea?"

Cassie smiled. "Sure," she said, "and it wouldn't hurt for us to brush your hair either."

Now that Cassie and Petey were in agreement about who was in charge, things would go smoothly, she thought happily. She was starting to feel better about the whole horse disaster that morning. At least now, she could keep her mind on something else besides her own failure.

First, Cassie put Sweet Pea in her stall and spent some time spiffing up Petey's appearance. His shirt had come untucked, and there was a spot of peanut butter on his front pocket. But that washed off with a little soap and water. Cassie also scrubbed Petey's face and hands.

"Hey, my mom doesn't scrub my face that hard," Petey sputtered.

"I'm not your mom," said Cassie, finishing her job.

Right now, she felt like his mother, and this little boy was not going to weasel out of a good cleaning.

"I don't want to be clean. I don't like the fair. I want to go home and play with my toys," said Petey.

"No way!" exclaimed Cassie. "Sweet Pea is counting on you. There. Now you look like a winner!"

Petey stopped protesting. He stood up taller and prouder. He looked at Sweet Pea.

"Baaa," said Sweet Pea.

Petey looked back at Cassie with a grin. "You really think me and Sweet Pea could win a ribbon?"

"I really think so," said Cassie, grinning. Her little cousin could be pretty cute when he wanted to be. She glanced at her watch. "Oh! Now let's hurry and get Sweet Pea ready. It's almost time for the competition."

Cassie, You're a Winner!

9

Somehow Cassie survived the next hour. She helped Petey practice walking Sweet Pea back and forth in the sheep barn. Sweet Pea was a cute lamb—loud, but cute. All in all, Cassie found herself enjoying being with Petey at his first fair. For a while, she almost forgot about Chester and choosing to miss her show that morning.

Aunt Mary just barely made it back from the hospital in time to see Petey show Sweet Pea. Cassie took photos so that Aunt Mary could enjoy the event. A few times, Cassie wasn't sure that Petey knew what to do with his lamb in the show ring. But he managed to wander around inside the arena with the lamb following him by the lead rope. The audience loved it.

"Oh, isn't that just the most adorable thing you've ever seen? A little boy and his lamb. What a precious picture," said an older woman sitting near Cassie.

It was true. Petey was a show-stealer! In fact, when the prizes were awarded, Petey and Sweet

Pea walked out with a second-place red ribbon. Cassie cheered with delight. Then she remembered her own failure. She swallowed hard. There would be no blue ribbon for Cassie in horseback riding.

Her cookie event was her remaining hope for a blue ribbon. On her way to the food pavilion later, she bumped smack into Iggy Potts! He had just finished a hot dog and was tossing the wrapper into a nearby garbage can.

"Come on, Cassie," he said between chews, grabbing her arm. He nearly pulled her all the way into the arts building. "Look! Two of my photos won blue ribbons, see? And this one got an honorable mention. That means even though it didn't place, it was still a good photograph."

"Oh Iggy, they're beautiful!" Cassie said. "I like this one best—of the countryside."

She touched one of the blue ribbons. "You deserve it. You are really talented, Iggy."

"Not too shabby, I'd say," teased Iggy with a silly but proud grin on his face. "So how about you? Sorry I missed your show. How did it go?"

Cassie's smile faded. Iggy instantly recognized that he had said the wrong thing.

"Not good," she said finally. "Chester freaked out over a starting gun for the car races. We never entered the show ring. We were both pretty shaken up, I guess."

Cassie, You're a Winner!

Iggy looked so sad he might cry. Good old Iggy. "Oh Cassie, I didn't know. I'm sorry. But hey, there's always next year. So let's get over there to your cookie event. Those good old stinky poodles are sure to win."

Cassie laughed in spite of her disappointment. She couldn't help it. When Iggy was around, a smile was always nearby.

Iggy grabbed his camera, and off they went to the food pavilion. It was packed with crowds of people waiting for the judges to select the winners of each youth exhibit.

Cassie watched as the three judges studied the recipe cards and inspected the coloring and texture of each cookie entry. They then smelled the cookies and each judge tasted one cookie from every entry. The judges were taking notes the whole time.

As Cassie watched, her family waved to her from across the room. Mom, Dad, Pat, Greta, and Aunt Mary were all there. Then Petey's head popped up, as he stood on a chair to see over the heads of the grown-ups. Cassie smiled. Now her time to shine was coming. She had been disappointed this morning, but that was over. She couldn't wait to see the judges' faces as they tasted her heaven-touched, prayed-over cookies.

Five minutes felt like five hours to Cassie. By the time the judges got to Cassie's Snickerdoodles Deluxe, she was trembling with anticipation. First, the judges read her original recipe. One of the judges, a lady in a purple dress, seemed quite impressed. She jotted a few notes on her notepad and exclaimed something about "originality." Cassie beamed. She glanced at her father, who winked at her and gave her the thumbs-up sign.

The judging of her cookies' texture and coloring seemed to go very well, too. Again, the lady in the purple dress remarked about how light the texture seemed. Then she said, "What a remarkable, beautiful golden cookie!"

During the judging, Iggy took one photograph after another. He whispered excitedly, "This is going great! Looks like you're a shoe-in for the big blue!"

Cassie could feel her heart rising into her throat. She could almost feel the silky blue ribbon fluttering against her hand. Just then, J.J. slipped in behind her and squeezed her arm. "Oh Cassie, this is it. I can feel it!" she whispered.

Cassie felt good having her friends there to support her, especially in such a shining moment of glory. Finally, she was being recognized for excellence and her family and friends were all there to witness it!

The time then came for the all-important taste test. The judges each took a cookie and bit in with great expectancy. Cassie held her breath, as smiles began to spread across the faces of each judge.

At that instant, the first judge coughed slightly. Then he sputtered, then puckered his like a goldfish, gasping for breath. "Water, please," he croaked.

Cassie, You're a Winner!

The second and third judges stopped chewing the cookies and looked at each other. The judge in the purple dress took out a handkerchief, covered her mouth, and appeared to spit out the contents. "Oh my," she said. "Such a contrast of flavors."

"Without a doubt, it's a fact," choked another judge. "A surprising aftertaste, indeed."

The first judge was still coughing loudly. "What are these cookies called again?" he managed to ask between coughs.

Cassie stood there mortified, speechless, empty.

Suddenly, a shrill little voice from the back of the room broke the silence. "I know! I know! They're Cassie's Snickerdoodles Deluxe, and I helped her bake them!"

10

Cassie knew that little voice.

She began to feel numb, hot, and cold—all at the same time. Her ears were ringing like a bell choir. A hundred pairs of eyes searched about for the owner of that cute little voice at the back of the room.

Petey stood perched on the chair and waved to everyone. He had the entire room's full attention. "That's my cousin, Cassie, over there. I helped her make Snickerdoodles," he said proudly.

Soft laughter filtered through the pavilion. An older woman standing nearby leaned toward her and whispered, "Isn't that the little boy who showed the lamb?"

"That's the one," said Cassie blankly. J.J. put her arm around Cassie's shoulder.

"What a cute little boy," said the woman.

Petey continued as if he had a speech of great public importance to deliver. "I went to Cassie's house last night. When Cassie took the dog outside, I mixed in the stuff she forgot."

Again, there was laughter. But Cassie didn't think it was funny.

"What stuff did I forget to put in the cookie dough, Petey?" Cassie heard herself say. All the people turned around and stared at her, but she no longer cared.

"My race car oil," said Petey. "I put it on the cookie pan. Then I poured some in the cookie dough too, to make it shiny. And some pickle juice. And some more of that powdery stuff."

"You mean a whole jar of cream of tartar?" Cassie demanded to know. She felt like she was a lawyer, and Petey was on trial for assault on a batch of her client's cookies.

"That tooth decay spice?" said Iggy, scrunching up the freckles on his nose.

J.J. gave him a look that meant, "Hush, before you go too far."

"Sorry," said Iggy, "I was just trying to lighten the moment."

Aunt Mary picked up Petey off the chair. "Oh, my darling boy. Pickle juice? Race car oil? A whole jar of cream of tartar? You couldn't have done all that to poor Cassie's cookies. You wouldn't! Tell Mommy you didn't do it!"

"But I did, Mommy. I helped Cassie make her cookies for the fair. But they taste nasty. I don't ever want any more Snickerdoodles!"

Cassie's mouth hung gaping like a codfish. She was

Cassie, You're a Winner!

ruined forever. There would be no blue ribbons at all now. On top of that, she was publicly humiliated in front of her friends, her family, perfect strangers, and even the judges. Cassie's Snickerdoodles Deluxe would go down in fair book history as the worst food entry ever entered in the Misty Falls Fair.

It didn't seem to matter who placed first, second, and third in the junior cookie baking exhibit. Cassie didn't stick around to find out. She just wanted to get as far away from the Misty Falls Fairgrounds as possible. Maybe she would just leave Misty Falls forever, if she could think of somewhere else to go.

But everywhere Cassie turned there were walls of people. She squeezed and squirmed her way through the crowds. Then someone gently touched her arm. "Before you go dear, there's something you need to know."

To Cassie's great surprise, it was one of the judges—the lady in the purple dress. She was smiling ever so tenderly. "Hello, Cassie. I'm Mrs. Reed. I must tell you that your recipe for Snickerdoodles is the best I've ever seen in my twenty-five years of judging and my forty-five years of cooking and baking. I'm delighted to know your secret for making the very best Snickerdoodles possible."

"But they taste terrible," said Cassie.

"Oh, but dear," said Mrs. Reed, "remember, it wasn't your fault, now was it? You had a little helper who got carried away! Now, you mustn't be discouraged, dear. That little bit of buttermilk and a smidgeon more cinnamon in your recipe is what has been missing in my own Snickerdoodles. You are quite a talented young cook! You remind me of myself at your age."

"Thank you," said Cassie meekly. She wasn't sure she believed Mrs. Reed's kind words. She still wanted to disappear off the face of the earth.

"My dear, I could tell you a tale about my first attempt at cooking. When I was twelve years old, I made the worst banana bread you've ever tasted in your life. I tried to feed it to our family dog, and he wouldn't even touch it," she said, laughing.

Cassie felt herself giggle. "You know, my dog Opie didn't want to eat my cookies either!"

The two of them laughed together. Then Mrs. Reed gave Cassie a big hug. Finally, Cassie lifted her head a little higher and smiled at the kind judge. "I'm sorry about the bitter cookie taste, Mrs. Reed. I didn't know. I thought—well, I prayed over those cookies, so I thought they would taste delicious today. That was silly."

"That's not silly at all, my dear," said Mrs. Reed. "My goodness, I pray over my cooking all the time! Now listen to me, Cassie. I believe God has given you a special talent, in fact, several special talents. Petey's mother just told me that you are his favorite cousin, and that you helped him place second in the lamb event this morning. You have a big heart and lots of talent. That's much more important than blue ribbons. And just because God didn't turn your cookies into delicious blue-ribbon cookies doesn't mean he didn't make you a good cook."

Amazed and dazed, Cassie still wasn't so sure about what Mrs. Reed was saying. "Thank you," she said with a smile. As Cassie turned to go, Mrs. Reed stopped her. "One more thing, Cassie. I was wondering if you could do the Misty Falls Community Church bloodmobile a huge favor this coming week."

"What?" asked Cassie, surprised.

"Yes, well, you see, our blood drive is going quite well, and we are nearly out of cookies. We need several dozen to finish out the week. As you know, people give blood for the local hospital to help patients. We feed the people who give blood to help rebuild their strength and thank them for their sacrifice."

"Oh, uh, how nice," Cassie stuttered.

"I hope you will consider baking your Snickerdoodles for our bloodmobile kitchen," said Mrs. Reed. "In fact, with your beautiful smile, we could use you to help serve the cookies this Tuesday, if you're available."

"This Tuesday?" asked Cassie, startled.

"Can I help, too?" asked Iggy, who was eavesdropping.

"Oh, how delightful!" exclaimed Mrs. Reed. "You can bring your camera with you and take pictures."

Adventures in Misty Falls

Before Cassie knew it, she had become a professional Snickerdoodle baker for the Misty Falls bloodmobile. In a matter of minutes, she didn't feel like moving away from Misty Falls anymore. In fact, she felt happy. Even more importantly, she felt needed.

That day, Cassie didn't go home from the fair with a single blue ribbon. But she did go home ready to bake cookies.

11

That afternoon, Iggy and J.J. stopped by just as the fragrance of freshly baked Snickerdoodles filled the kitchen at Cassie's house.

"Mmm," said J.J., breathing in a whiff. "Are they ready yet?"

Iggy didn't ask. He just grabbed a cookie off the cooling rack before Cassie could object.

"Help yourself," laughed Cassie.

After Iggy and J.J. had eaten all the Snickerdoodles and drunk all the milk their stomachs could hold, Iggy winked at J.J. "Alright J.J., you know what to do," he said slyly.

J.J. pulled a scarf out of her pocket, blindfolded Cassie, and seated her in a chair at the breakfast table. "Hey," said Cassie, "what's going on?"

"Iggy, what's going on?" Cassie demanded to know. She could hear them both giggling and whispering about something. Someone opened the back door, and soon something rattled mysteriously.

Finally, J.J. began untying the scarf. She announced, "Alright Cassie, you may look."

As the scarf fell from Cassie's eyes, she spotted a package on the table, wrapped in blue paper. "What is it?" Cassie asked, confused. She examined the faces of her friends for a clue.

"Open it," said Iggy proudly.

"Yes, hurry, Cassie!" J.J. urged as she shifted from foot to foot eagerly.

Cassie ripped open the blue paper. Inside was a framed picture. Cassie gasped. The picture was of a girl with flowing hair, gallantly riding Chester at a full gallop. It almost looked like J.J., except the girl had light auburn hair.

"Where did you get this?" Cassie asked.

Iggy smiled. "I told you that you and Chester were awesome yesterday."

"You mean—this is me?" Cassie cried. She couldn't believe it. When Chester had bolted from the sound of that starting gun, Cassie had never felt so clumsy trying to ride a horse. But here in the picture, she looked— well, graceful. And Chester was handsome, too!

"It's you, Cassie," said J.J., reaching out to hug her friend.

All at once, Cassie fell in love with Chester again. She just kept staring at the picture, unable to speak.

Then Iggy said, "There's more, Cass. Turn the picture frame over."

Cassie, You're a Winner!

When Cassie obeyed, there, taped to the back of the frame, was a blue ribbon.

"Oh Iggy!"

"Remember when I left you suddenly yesterday? Well, Dad and I hurried and developed the photos I took of you and Chester," Iggy said excitedly. "Today, I showed it at the fair in another exhibit, and it won, Cassie! You have your blue ribbon. It's yours. You worked hard for it. You've earned it."

Cassie felt the satiny blue ribbon. She wasn't sure what to say. "I can't take this," Cassie said finally. "After all, Iggy, it was your talent that won you the ribbon. Not mine."

Iggy's face fell with disappointment. "But it's yours."

Cassie looked at J.J. She had that "don't-argue-with-me" look on her face. Iggy was turning shades of purple. Cassie began to smile, and then her smile turned into laughter. Soon, J.J. and Iggy were laughing, too.

"You guys are the best," said Cassie. "But I don't really care about winning blue ribbons anymore."

"Why? What happened?" asked J.J. "Did you change your mind?"

"No," Cassie said. "I think God changed my mind. In a funny sort of way, He showed me that blue ribbons don't really matter all that much. They're nice to earn, but that's not what makes a person special. It's just being the way God made me that makes me special."

J.J. grinned. "Here, let me help you with the next batch of cookies."

"Great," said Cassie. "Just think, our cookies are going to help someone at the bloodmobile on Tuesday."

Iggy took another big bite out of the biggest Snickerdoodle left on the cooling rack.

"Do ya think I could help eat the stinky poodles at the bloodmobile?"

"You're already doing a good job of eating them now!" exclaimed Cassie.

Never had Cassie had so much fun baking before. It was more than fun, it was a celebration.

After Iggy and J.J. left, Cassie hung the picture that Iggy had given her in her room over her bed. That night, as she lay in bed, Cassie stared at the stars through the open window. Next to the picture was the blue ribbon, fluttering in the night breeze.

Cassie almost giggled as she thought about how God had chosen to answer her prayers. He surely had not answered in the way she expected. But He had shown her through Mrs. Reed, her friends, and even through Petey that she was special. Cassie couldn't wait to serve her Snickerdoodles at the bloodmobile.

"Thank you, Lord," she whispered. "I never want to go through this again. But thank you for the good day, just the same."

Cassie, You're a Winner!

She listened in the stillness of her room, as the crickets outside chirped. She could almost hear God say,
"Cassie Marie Holbrook is special to Me, stinky poodles, bumpy skin, and all."

A Letter From the Author

Dear Friend,

Welcome to the Misty Falls Club!

We're just starting our Adventures in Misty Falls series, so you've picked a great time to join us. I hope you've enjoyed reading *Cassie, You're A Winner!* I really enjoy writing about Cassie, because she reminds me of someone who is near and dear to my heart—my youngest child, Mary-Alison. And I have to admit, I was a lot like Cassie when I was growing up.

If you enjoyed getting to know Cassie, J.J., and Iggy in this book, you're going to love what you find in our next book, *Best Friends Forever?*, available in Christian bookstores everywhere. Check out our Web site, www.mistyfallsfriends.com. You'll find lots more fun information about Cassie and the rest of the Misty Falls gang.

Happy Reading!

BEST FRIENDS FOREVER?

Whether Cassie always likes it or not, her life is full of unexpected surprises. In *Best Friends Forever?*, her adventures continue. Find out what happens when she makes more of her famous Snickerdoodles, Iggy faints, and her best friend J.J. grows closer to a sweet, but unusual, new friend.

Will Cassie feel left out forever in the big, cold world without her best friend?

Look for this next exciting adventure in the Misty Falls series at your local Christian bookstore.

Book 2:
"Adventures in Misty Falls" series
Best Friends Forever?
N007117
$4.99 • 1-56309-734-6 • Paper

Best Friends Forever?
1-56309-734-6
N007117
$4.99

BEST FRIENDS FOREVER?

RENÉE KENT

Cassie wasn't so sure how the afternoon would turn out. With every second that ticked by, her stomach was growing tighter. What if she couldn't think of anything to say to the boys and girls she met? She always felt a little awkward around new people.

It was too late to turn back now. They were already at the New Hope Center.

The New Hope Center was a place where children stayed who had been released from the hospital but weren't quite healthy enough to go home yet. Cassie, J.J., and Iggy had agreed to come to New Hope Center to visit one of the sick children who didn't get to see her family very often.

They walked through the front door of the New Hope Center and went down the hall. Nurse Trixie led them to a door with a handmade sign that read, "Robyn's Room."

Nurse Trixie knocked.

"Come in," piped a sweet, soft voice. A tiny girl with a head full of short blonde hair busily typed on a computer at her desk. The girl looked up and grinned widely. "Oh! I have company!" she chirped.

"I'm tired of resting," Robyn continued, making a funny face. "I've been lying around for months, and I'm ready for action!"

Robyn smiled as she looked right into Cassie's eyes. Cassie found herself staring uncomfortably at her own dirty sneakers. But J.J. met Robyn's smile with a toothy grin in return.

Robyn touched the red feathers in J.J.'s hair clasp. "These are beautiful. Are they real?" She asked.

"Yes, but they're dyed that color," said J.J. "It was a gift from my father. He lives in Arizona. My Navajo grandmother made it. My father gave it to me for my birthday a long time ago."

"It's very pretty against your long, black hair, J.J.," Robyn said, crossing her legs in the big chair. "So you don't live with your father, either."

"No," said J.J. "My parents are divorced. I live with my mother here in Georgia now. But Robyn, where is your dad?"

Robyn's eyes softened. "He's in heaven with my mom. We were in a car accident when I was little."

Cassie's heart felt broken and amazed for Robyn, and J.J. too.

Best Friends Forever?

J.J. had never talked about her parents' divorce before, Cassie thought to herself. Just now, it seemed easy, almost too easy, for J.J. to share her thoughts with Robyn.

As soon as they had piled into the car after their visit with Robyn, J.J. was a regular chatterbox. "I just love Robyn, don't you? Isn't she cute?"

Cassie felt a little like crying.

"Hey, I know what we can do," said J.J. "Let's plan to keep Robyn busy between now and the time she goes home from New Hope Center. We could get a ride over there every other day or so."

"Great," said Cassie blandly. Inside she was thinking, "Why should I go? Robyn is J.J.'s new best friend, not mine."

J.J., Navajo Princess
1-56309-763-X
N007105
$4.99

Address: http://www.mistyfallsfriends.com

Back | Forward | Stop | Refresh | Home | Search | Mail | Favorites

A WHOLE NEW MISTY FALLS WORLD IS READY FOR YOU TO EXPLORE ON THE WEB!

What do Cassie and the gang do in their spare time?

What games do they like to play?

What's going on at Misty Falls Middle School?

What does Misty Falls look like?

**Visit
www.mistyfallsfriends.com
to find out!**

ADVENTURES IN MISTY FALLS

Don't miss any of the adventures of Cassie and the Misty Falls gang.

Read all the books!

☐ **Cassie, You're a Winner!**
1-56309-735-4
N007116
$4.99 retail price
$1.99 through 12/31/00

☐ **Best Friends Forever?**
1-56309-734-6
N007117
$4.99

☐ **J.J., Navajo Princess**
1-56309-763-X
N007105
$4.99

☐ **Robyn Flies Home**
1-56309-764-8
N007106
$4.99

Look for books 5 and 6—available in October 2000!